The Log of Christopher Columbus

by CHRISTOPHER COLUMBUS

selections by STEVE LOWE

illustrations by ROBERT SABUDA

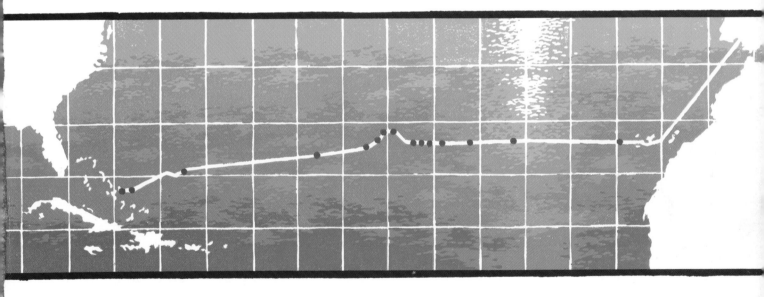

The First Voyage: Spring, Summer and Fall 1492

PHILOMEL BOOKS · NEW YORK

Columbus

To my mother and father,
who told me never to look back.
– R.S.

Grateful acknowledgment is made to *The Log of Christopher Columbus*
by Robert H. Fuson, whose careful research provided the text for this book.
Fuson's words are used in their entirety, and any deletions are carefully
noted by ellipses. The only alteration to his text is the spelling out
of the four directions where his abbreviations appeared.
Fuson's words are from two sources. The first is the Las Casas's
transcription of the Admiral's original Castilian log, which exists today
in Madrid's National Library. His second source comes from portions of
Columbus's first biography, written by his son Ferdinand.

The illustrator would like to thank The Peabody Museum of Salem for its
assistance and guidance in the research of the illustrations for this book.

Compilation copyright © 1992 by Steven Lowe. Illustrations copyright © 1992 by Robert Sabuda.
Excerpted, with permission, from book #60660 *The Log of Christopher Columbus*, by Robert H. Fuson,
copyright 1987 by Robert H. Fuson. Published by International Marine, a Division of TAB BOOKS Inc.,
Blue Ridge Summit, Pennsylvania 17294 (1-800-233-1128 or 717-794-2191). All rights reserved.
This book, or parts thereof, may not be reproduced in any form without permission in writing from the publisher.
Published by Philomel Books, a division of The Putnam & Grosset Book Group,
200 Madison Avenue, New York, NY 10016. Published simultaneously in Canada.
Printed in Hong Kong by South China Printing Co. (1988) Ltd.
Book design by Gunta Alexander. The text was set in Schneidler.
Library of Congress Cataloging-in-Publication Data
Lowe, Steve. The log of Christopher Columbus / by Steve Lowe; illustrated by Robert Sabuda.
p. cm. Summary: A simple adaptation of excerpts in Columbus's diary,
from his departure from Spain to his landing in the New World in 1492.
1. Columbus, Christopher–Juvenile literature. 2. America–Discovery and exploration–Spanish–
Juvenile literature. 3. Explorers–America–Juvenile literature. 4. Explorers–Spain–Juvenile literature.
[1. Columbus, Christopher–Diaries. 2. Explorers–Diaries. 3. America–Discovery and exploration–Spanish.
4. Diaries.] I. Sabuda, Robert, ill.] II. Columbus, Christopher. Diario. English. III. Title.
E118.L69 1992 970.01′5–dc20 91-17156 CIP AC ISBN 0-399-22139-5
1 3 5 7 9 10 8 6 4 2
First Impression

INTRODUCTION

Years before Columbus set sail to change the course of history, he wrote these words in a favorite geography book: "The end of Spain and the beginning of India are not far distant but close, and it is evident that this sea is navigable in a few days with a fair wind." While others believed this too, Columbus was determined to prove it.

Columbus had the dream of sailing west to India, but not the money. Turned down once by King John of Portugal and once at the court of Spain, he made a last appeal to Ferdinand and Isabella: Pay my expenses, then name me Admiral of the not-so-wide ocean, and I will bring you back the gold of India.

In the spring of 1492 the king and queen agreed.

With his reputation at stake, Columbus set about the task of proving what he believed. A fair wind, he thought, might be had off the western coast of Africa, far south of the Azores. There in the Canaries, he guessed, were the westward currents that would send his small fleet to Marco Polo's fabulously rich Indies in less than thirty days.

By the time the Niña, the Pinta, and the Santa Maria had covered all the miles Columbus believed separated Europe from India, he was still a week away from land. He used no maps, no instrument but a compass. He lied about the distance traveled to angry sailors who no longer trusted him. He pushed the crew westward, dreading that he might have passed land at night. He offered a reward to whoever spotted land first, then threatened punishment if the sighting proved false. He even began to wonder if he imagined land where there was only horizon. Then, after sailing thirty-three days without sight of land, Christopher Columbus kept three frightened crews from mutiny for two more days—the time it took to follow migrating birds to the moonlit beach of a new world.

No one knows how many brave mariners never returned from attempts to cross the Atlantic before Columbus. What we do know is that in 1492–1493, a crew of ninety led by Christopher Columbus left Europe, made contact with a new continent to the west, and returned. We know this because Columbus wrote a daily log Although the original log is missing today, copies of it were made in the sixteenth century. So the words you read here are as close to Columbus's own as we will ever have.

—Steve Lowe
Summer 1991

Spring and summer 1492

*B*ased on the information that I had given Your Highnesses about the land of India…Your Highnesses decided to send me, Christopher Columbus, to the regions of India, to see the princes there and the peoples and the lands.

I left Grenada on Saturday, the twelfth day of the month of May in the same year of 1492 and went to the town of Palos, which is a seaport. There I fitted out three vessels, very suited to such an enterprise. I left the said port well supplied with a large quantity of provisions and with many seamen on the third day of the month of August in the said year, on a Friday, half an hour before sunrise. I set my course for the Canary Islands of Your Highnesses, which are in the Ocean Sea, from there to embark on a voyage that will last until I arrive in the Indies.…I decided to write down everything I might do and see and experience on this voyage, from day to day, and very carefully.

Thursday September 6, 1492

Shortly before noon I sailed from the harbor at Gomera and set my course to the west.

Sunday September 9, 1492

This day we completely lost sight of
land, and many men sighed and wept
for fear they would not see it again for
a long time. I comforted them with
great promises of lands and riches. To
sustain their hope and dispel their fears
of a long voyage, I decided to reckon
fewer leagues than we actually made.
I did this that they might not think
themselves so great a distance from
Spain as they really were. For myself
I will keep a confidential accurate
reckoning.

Saturday September 15, 1492

I sailed to the west day and night for 81 miles, or more. Early this morning I saw a marvelous meteorite fall into the sea 12 or 15 miles to the southwest. This was taken by some people to be a bad omen, but I calmed them by telling of the numerous occasions that I have witnessed such events. I have to confess that this is the closest that a falling star has ever come to my ship.

Monday September 17, 1492

I held my course to the west and made, day and night, 150 miles or more, but I only logged 141 miles....I saw a great deal of weed today – weed from rocks that lie to the west. I take this to mean that we are near land....Everyone is cheerful, and the *Pinta*, the fastest sailing vessel, went ahead as fast as it could in order to sight land.

Tuesday September 18, 1492

...*I* have sailed for 11 days under a full sail, running ever before the wind....

Wednesday September 19, 1492

The wind of last night has left us....It is my desire to go directly to the Indies and not get sidetracked with islands that I shall see on the return passage, God willing. The weather is good.

Thursday September 20, 1492

Today I changed course for the first time since departing Gomera because the wind was variable and sometimes calm....Very early this morning three little birds flew over the ship, singing as they went, and flew away as the sun rose. This was a comforting thought, for unlike the large water birds, these little birds could not have come from far off.

Friday September 21, 1492

Today was mostly calm….The sea is as smooth as a river….

Sunday September 23, 1492

I saw a dove, a tern, another small river bird, and some white birds….The crew is still grumbling about the wind. When I get a wind from the southwest or west it is inconstant, and that, along with a flat sea, has led the men to believe that we will never get home.

Monday September 24, 1492

I am having serious trouble with the crew....All day long and all night long those who are awake and able to get together never cease to talk to each other in circles, complaining that they will never be able to return home. They have said that it is insanity and suicidal on their part to risk their lives following the madness of a foreigner....Some feel that they have already arrived where men have never dared to sail and that they are not obliged to go to the end of the world....I am told by a few trusted men (and these are few in number!) that if I persist in going onward, the best course of action will be to throw me into the sea some night.

Tuesday September 25, 1492

At sunset Martín mounted the stern
of the *Pinta* and with great joy called
to me that he saw land and claimed
the reward. When I heard this stated
so positively, I fell to my knees to give
thanks to Our Lord....My people did
the same thing, and the *Niña's* crew all
climbed the mast and rigging, and all
claimed that it was land.

Wednesday September 26, 1492

After sunrise I realized that what we all thought was land last evening was nothing more than squall clouds, which often resemble land. I returned to my original course of west in the afternoon, once I was positive that what I had seen was not land. Day and night I sailed 93 miles, but recorded 72. The sea was like a river and the air sweet and balmy.

Monday October 1, 1492

*I*t rained very hard this morning.…
My personal calculation shows that we
have come 2121 miles. I did not reveal
this figure to the men because they
would become frightened, finding
themselves so far from home, or at least
thinking that they were that far.

Sunday October 7, 1492

This morning we saw what appeared to be land to the west, but it was not very distinct. Furthermore, no one wished to make a false claim of discovery, for I had ordered that if anyone make such a claim and, after sailing three days, the claim proved to be false, the…reward promised by the Catholic Sovereigns would be forfeited, even if afterwards he actually did see it. Being warned of this, no one aboard the *Santa María* or *Pinta* dared call out "Land, land."

…Joy turned to dismay as the day progressed, for by evening we had found no land and had to face the reality that it was only an illusion.

Thursday October 11, 1492

About 10 o'clock at night, while standing on the sterncastle, I thought I saw a light to the west. It looked like a little wax candle bobbing up and down....I am the first to admit that I was so eager to find land that I did not trust my own senses, so I called for Pedro Gutiérrez, the representative of the King's household, and asked him to watch for the light. After a few moments, he too saw it.

Friday October 12, 1492

The moon, in its third quarter, rose in the east shortly before midnight.... Then, at two hours after midnight, the *Pinta* fired a cannon....I hauled in all sails but the mainsail and lay-to till daylight. The land is about 6 miles to the west.

Friday October 12, 1492

*A*t dawn…I went ashore in the ship's boat. I unfurled the royal banner. After a prayer of thanksgiving I ordered the captains of the *Pinta* and the *Niña*…to bear faith and witness that I was taking possession of this island for the King and Queen….To this island I gave the name *San Salvador*….

No sooner had we concluded the formalities of taking possession of the island than people began to come to the beach, all as naked as their mothers bore them….They are very well-built people…their eyes are large and very pretty….Many of the natives paint their faces…others paint their whole bodies….They are friendly….

Tuesday November 27, 1492

As I went along the river it was marvelous to see the forests and greenery, the very clear water, the birds, and the fine situation, and I almost did not want to leave the place. I told the men with me that, in order to make a report to the Sovereigns of the things they saw, a thousand tongues would not be sufficient to tell it, nor my hand to write it, for it looks like an enchanted land.

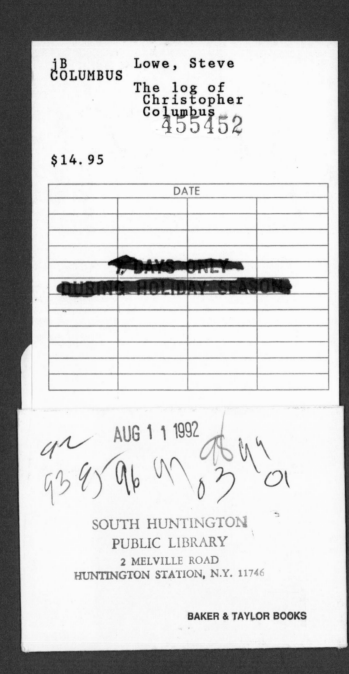